What real kids like you are saying about the Wright on Time books:

"When I first read *Wright on Time: Arizona* and this book, the thing that I loved was the *Mystery*! I think it's great that you came up with 'The Mysterious Device' and how it will keep everyone on their heels. I can't wait for the next book!"

— **Chas** from Washington, age 11

"I totally enjoyed these characters and I learned a lot about what's really inside a cave. Can't wait for the next adventure!"

— **Brooke** from Alabama, age 8

"The *Wright on Time* family was the most awesome family ever! The caves and gems were so cool. I can't wait for their next adventure."

— **Xianne** from Iowa, age 6

"I really like the book and I really want to go mining now! I want to visit a real cave! The facts in the book help me at school, too. I liked when the kids found real gems in the cave. I hope they find lots of dinosaur bones in Utah."

— **Adam** from Arizona, age 8

"It's wicked freaky awesome, Mumma! Thank you for getting me a book about kids like me!"

— **Lochlann** from New Hampshire, age 5 ¾

"I like Arizona. It is cool, exciting AND interesting. I like the part about the soda straws!"

— **Sebastian** from Massachusetts, age 10

"YES! Like book!"

— **Aidan** from Massachusetts, age 2

"Your book is awesome. It's so cool. I love it. I can't wait until the next one comes out. I'm sure it's going to be awesome!"

— **Jacqueline** from Arizona, age 9 ½

"I finished reading the book last night I could not stop reading it. ☺ I loved the book and I am looking forward to the next one."

— **Melissa** from Arizona, age 11

Lisa M. Cottrell-Bentley

Wright on Time™

UTAH

Illustrations by Tanja Bauerle

ISBN: 0-9824829-1-4
ISBN-13: 9780982482919
Library of Congress Control Number: 2009939034

Visit www.WrightOnTimeBooks.com to order additional copies.

To my beautiful and talented daughter
Teagan
who brought the humor to these books
and *always* makes me smile

Egyptian Symbol - travel freely

UTAH

Utah became a State on January 4th, 1896

Blue Spruce
State Tree

California Sea Gull
State Bird

Rocky Mountain Elk
State Animal

Allosaurus
State Fossil

Sego Lily
State Flower

The Beehive State
State Nickname

Honey Bee
State Insect

Logan

Great Salt Lake

Ogden

Salt Lake City
State Capital

Provo

King's Peak
13,528 ft.

Copper
State Mineral

Zion National Park

Bryce Canyon National Park

Arches National Park

Lake Powell

Chapter One

Dear Connor,

It's been 38 days now since we left home. I miss you a lot. We've had a lot of fun though. My sister is helping me write this e-mail while we wait for Mom to finish working for the day and for Dad to finish with the laundry in the campground's laundry room.

We're in Utah now. Since it's June, it isn't cold here but there is still snow on the top of the mountains. I was hoping to see snow. We've been here about a week and we leave in another week to go to South Dakota. On the way here we went to the Grand Canyon, the Barringer Crater, the Petrified Forest, and Four Corners — which is the only place in the entire United States where four states all meet together. We saw petroglyphs in a couple of places, a bunch of freaky cool rock arches, a bunch of oil derricks, and a statue of a guy standing on a corner in Winslow, Arizona. It wasn't in that order though. We've officially only been to four states so far: Arizona, New Mexico, Utah, and Colorado. But, we only just stepped on New Mexico and Colorado at Four Corners. My favorite thing so far has been the crater. It's so big! I wish we could have explored there more. Did you get my postcard from there?

We've been swimming a lot here at the campground. In the afternoons, we've been going to this dinosaur dig. Nadia and I haven't found any bones and we probably won't, but we've been able to watch and help the paleontologists uncover parts of an Allosaurus fragilis. Apparently it's Utah's state dinosaur. I asked the paleontologists at the dig what Arizona's state dinosaur is, but I haven't found out

UTAH

yet. Nadia is telling me now that she'll look it up for me as soon as we send this e-mail. I hope it has a state dinosaur. Not all states do!

Did you get the package I sent with the iron pyrite from the cave in Arizona and the crater dust? Try using a magnet on the crater dust. It's really neat.

E-mail me back soon!
Your best friend,
Aidan

"Well, that's about it. I think we've e-mailed everyone," eleven year old Nadia Wright said to her seven year old brother Aidan.

"I think so," Aidan replied.

Just then their dad, Harrison, stepped into the Wright family's RV home carrying a large canvas duffle bag filled with their clean clothes. "I'm home!" he declared to the room.

"Yay!" Aidan hollered. He started to hug his dad, but the bag got in the way. Harrison set it on the couch and gave Aidan a huge hug.

Nadia stood up from the laptop and reached over to grab some of the clean clothes to put away.

"So, who's ready to go to the dino-dig?" Harrison asked.

"I am!" Aidan said.

"Me, too!" Nadia said.

Their mother, Stephanie, heard them from the bedroom in the back. She popped her head around the doorframe and said, "I'll be ready in about five minutes. I just need to finish debugging the program I've been working on."

Stephanie was a computer programmer who telecommuted while the family traveled around the United States. Their adventures were just beginning and living in a recreational vehicle gave them the freedom to roam as they pleased. They all loved the flexibility her job gave them and they were picking their travel locations based on various freelance writing jobs Harrison received as well as where they themselves wanted to go next. The children were homeschooled, and Aidan insisted they call it *roadschooled* until they moved back to their rented out home in Arizona.

"Prince Pumpkin the Third," Aidan said as he went to their pet turtle's terrarium, "we're going on another adventure today!" He stroked the top of the turtle's head.

The turtle stretched his neck in greeting.

UTAH

"Will Maeve and Arte Smith be arriving today?" Nadia asked her dad.

"Yes, they will. They meant to get here last week before us, but Maeve's work held them up. They were in Washington, D.C. for a linguistics symposium and apparently some researchers from abroad had a new runestone of some kind they wanted her to see. I'm not sure where they found it, but I guess it was important enough to keep Maeve's attention."

Nadia knew she had met her dad's scientist friends before, but she was the same age Aidan now was when it had happened and didn't really remember them. Four years is a long time when you are eleven years old.

"I'm glad they're coming now," said Nadia. "I'd like to try and get Maeve to help us figure out what the new symbols are on our mysterious device we found in the cave in Arizona. It's so cool that the symbols seem to change. I know one is definitely Chinese, but my research isn't bringing up any specific results for what it means."

"And the turtle symbol that was on it first is definitely Mayan, but not quite like anything I've found in the ancient stone markings," replied Harrison.

Stephanie had gone back to her work, but overheard them talking. It was hard to keep anything secret when you lived in a four-hundred square foot house. "Don't forget the new Egyptian symbol," she felt compelled to add in.

"I'm not so sure it is Egyptian," replied Nadia in a slightly louder voice. "I think it might also be Mayan or Native American. But, maybe you're right. It isn't as round as the other one. I just don't know. I can't wait to see what Maeve has to say."

"You're right," Harrison added. "It looks almost identical to the petroglyph we saw at Newspaper Rock in the Petrified Forest."

"There they go again," Aidan said to their pet turtle, Prince Pumpkin the Third. "And I thought we were here to find dinosaurs."

"Don't worry." Harrison smiled at Aidan as he put the folded dish towels in a kitchen drawer. "There's time for both."

"There'd better be," said Nadia with a smile. She knew her parents always made time for her and Aidan to do the things they wanted to do, but deciphering glyphs and digging up dinosaur bones both took a long time. They only had one more week before they planned to move on to South Dakota.

The three became simultaneously quiet. They could hear Stephanie's fingers clicking away at her keyboard.

UTAH

Harrison and Nadia finished folding the laundry as Aidan fed the turtle a snack of romaine lettuce and peas. This was Prince Pumpkin the Third's favorite meal. Aidan snuck a few peas for himself as well. Peas were one of his favorite foods too, especially cold ones.

The distinctive tone from Stephanie's computer shutting down let them know Mom was done working for the day. She quickly joined them in the living area.

"I'm ready. How about you?" Stephanie asked.

"We just need to grab the snacks and water," Harrison said.

With their cooler full, the Wright family locked up their RV and hopped into their little two door silver car. Within minutes they were off to their next adventure.

Chapter Two

Eastern Utah was hot and dry on this June day. The Wrights stumbled out of their car and tightly strapped on their hats. The frequent gusts of wind were sometimes powerful.

Nadia squinted. "Wish I'd thought to bring sunglasses," she commented.

"We will all have to remember them tomorrow," said Stephanie.

They walked toward the dig site they'd been working at and found Robert, the paleontologist in charge.

"Good afternoon!" Robert said to the Wright family as he caught up with them. "Guess what!" He looked to Aidan. "We found a furcula this morning."

"Furcula?" Nadia interrupted. "Isn't that a wishbone?"

"It sure is!" Robert smiled.

"But, how can a dinosaur have a furcula? I thought only birds had those," Nadia asked.

Robert looked at Aidan. The two of them had spent a lot of time together over the past week and they had become quite a team. Aidan loved learning about dinosaurs and was a natural at carefully digging for bones. Robert appreciated Aidan's deep interest and love for his work.

Aidan knew the answer to Nadia's question. "The Allosaurus is special," he said. "Most paleontologists believe that since the Allosaurus has a furcula it might be related to birds."

"But, I thought only animals who could fly had furculas," said Nadia.

"You'd think so, but not all because some dinosaurs had them, too," Aidan said.

"That's really neat. What other dinosaurs had wishbones?" Nadia asked Aidan as they followed Robert to the dig site.

UTAH

"The T-Rex does! Isn't that freaky cool?" Aidan said.

"Sure is," Nadia said.

"Some people think the Tyrannosaurus Rex is more closely related to hummingbirds than to other dinosaurs like the Triceratops."

"Wow, I had no idea."

Robert's big strides were hard for the kids to keep up with, so they ran to catch up.

A half dozen graduate students were working hard in the heat. Tan canvas make-shift huts polka-dotted the rocky landscape. Rope enclosed grids were in every area, both inside the huts and outside in the open. The posts holding the ropes had letters and numbers written on them in black ink to distinguish the different dig sites. The red dirt covered everything, even the people. Distinct white areas could be seen as they looked around. The white looked like snow, but was actually rock and dirt. A bright blue portable potty could be seen in the distance.

"Here it is! One of my assistants from the university found it. Her name is Amanda Prachett and she's already agreed to let your family help uncover it."

"Wow! This is so freaky awesome! Thanks, Amanda!" Aidan replied.

Amanda smiled back and handed Aidan a pick and a brush. "Dr. Robert says you are an experienced paleontologist-in-training, so I don't need to tell you how to do this."

"Nope, no need to brush up on that! Now I've got a bone to pick," Aidan answered with a smile. He had already begun. He was being very careful to only pick the area around the gray-black fossilized bone. The grid of ropes which mapped out the dig site made it a little more difficult to maneuver since it required the paleontologists to squat.

"Has this bone already been documented?" Aidan asked. He knew it was important to keep track of where every single bone was found and in what direction it was pointing. Those clues helped determine what had happened to that specific dinosaur or group of dinosaurs.

"It has," Amanda said. "The team artist was by just a few minutes ago making updates. She's been busy going around to all the dig sites today. It's been a very productive day for us."

"Freaky cool!" Aidan said.

"The furcula seems really fragile," Nadia noted as she bent down to examine the digging.

"It is," Robert said.

"Why is this bone so fragile when we've seen so many that are as solid as a rock?" Nadia asked.

"Good question," Robert said. "It all depends on how the bone was preserved. If the bone was in dirt and newly exposed to air, we'll sometimes cover it with a plaster wrap. We have to be really careful with the bones that haven't petrified. Petrified means..."

"Turned into rock," Aidan interrupted.

"Exactly right," Robert said.

"Since this furcula is not petrified, it is extremely delicate and could easily break. I'll be covering it in a plaster mix to help keep it from drying out once the entire bone is uncovered," Amanda added to the conversation.

"Plaster?" Stephanie asked. "Wouldn't that harm the bone?"

"It might seem so at first, but it actually keeps it safe. When it's time, the plaster comes off very easily. We first cover the bone in newspaper, then spray it with water.

Then, we cover it with burlap which has been dipped in plaster. The plaster dries extremely hard. Then, the bone can be transported without any harm coming to it. This is especially important for really large bones, like skulls and leg bones," Amanda said.

"It's also really important to do when it is only partially uncovered and we won't be getting back to it for a while," Robert added.

Robert's walkie-talkie made a crackling noise. He took it off his waistband and talked into it for a minute.

"Amanda and I have to go down to the main site at the tin hut," Robert said to the Wrights. "Since you're set, I'm sure you'll be fine. I'll check back in periodically. You can always walkie-talkie me if you need anything," he added as he made sure Harrison had his walkie-talkie on.

Amanda and Robert left. The Wright family situated their things and themselves and set back to work. Since this was a private dig site, they had the privilege of helping as much as the owner and caretakers allowed. This particular site was owned by a family who encouraged various colleges and professors to dig for research. They also funded all the work being done. The Wrights were surprised to learn that many private projects such as

UTAH

this one were paid for by individuals, rather than by the government or universities. Nadia and Aidan had fun discussing what projects they would fund in the future. If this dinosaur dig had been on federal or state land, they might not have been allowed to help and that made them sad. They dreamed of funding family-friendly projects all over the country some day.

Harrison had been invited to bring his family to this dig by his friend, Dr. Robert James, a paleontologist. Since Harrison was a freelance writer, he welcomed the idea of traveling around the country, spending time with his family and researching future articles at the same time. He was currently writing an article about dinosaur dig vacationing in Utah. Harrison's writing career was one of the main reasons that pushed the family to start their traveling adventure.

"You know," Nadia said to no one in particular a good while later, "digging was fun for a day or two, but I'm getting pretty bored of it after a week. I don't think this type of field work is for me."

Aidan, who wasn't even slightly bored, said, "You could go and help classify the bone fragments that haven't been matched to a particular species yet."

"Good idea," Stephanie said.

"Yeah," Nadia replied. "I think I will."

"I'll go with you," said Stephanie. "I get stiff sitting here brushing away dirt for too long."

"Okay, have fun," Harrison said as he glanced at his watch, "but Nadia and I have to leave in an hour to get to the airport in time to pick up Arte and Maeve."

"We'll be back by then," Stephanie said as she and Nadia stretched up. She tousled Aidan's curly brown hair and kissed him on the top of his head. The two then walked toward the tin hut where the classification computers were kept. A combination of solar and gas generators kept the computers and other necessary equipment powered.

Harrison and Aidan continued to work, slowly and carefully uncovering the Allosaurus furcula. They knew they might never get to see the fossil completely uncovered, but they were happy to be part of the process.

Robert was soon back to help with the digging. He enjoyed keeping the two company.

"How long does it usually take to uncover a bone this size?" Harrison asked.

Robert smiled as Aidan answered the question. "It depends on the soil, the weather, the condition of the

UTAH

bone, and the exact shape of the bone. For this furcula bone, my guess is about a week."

"Wow! That's spot on, Aidan," Robert said, with his English accent peeking through. "Normally it would be about a week. It'll probably actually take between ten days and two weeks since we have inexperienced people working on it," Robert joked.

"Oh, thanks," Aidan said in a mock sarcastic tone. After a week, they'd gotten in the habit of joking together a lot.

"I'm talking about the students," Robert whispered conspiratorially. He winked and whispered again, "No, they're all great of course, but none of you are as quick as I am."

With one expert clink of Robert's pick into the surrounding rock, they completely agreed. Harrison and Aidan watched Robert's moves with awe.

Harrison had his mind in two places, however, as he glanced at his watch and realized it was time to go to the airport to pick up the two experts who just might be able to help them solve the mystery of their strange device.

Chapter Three

"Off to the airport we go," Harrison said to Nadia and Robert. There would be just enough room for Arte and Maeve in their small five person car.

"I can't get over how quiet this car is," Robert said to Harrison. "Are all electric cars this quiet?"

"Yes, they are."

"How's it working for you?"

"We've been really happy with it. We've never driven a long ways with it. But for sight-seeing and shopping, it's been the ideal car. We certainly can't beat the gas mileage."

Robert laughed. "Can you put gas in it?"

"Most you can, but this one is special. We're actually testing it. It's a one-of-a-kind test vehicle which doesn't even have a gasoline tank. I'm writing a series of articles about how well it works for a family over the course of a year. It's been a lot of fun driving it. It's even more special since it is a very light car made from a special fiberglass and special metal alloy."

"You certainly won't need any of the stuff that comes out of those," Robert said as he pointed out the window at the hundreds of oil derricks they were passing by.

"No, we won't," Harrison said with a smile.

"It's funny that the crude oil out there was actually made from prehistoric zooplankton and algae," Nadia said. "Between that and the dinosaur bones, ancient creatures surround us here."

Nadia stared off into the distance, appreciating the beautiful Utah landscape. She especially enjoyed seeing the different types of mountains, the rocky red ones and the pine covered snowy ones.

By the time they got to the small airport, Nadia could hardly contain her excitement. She couldn't wait to show off their mystery device.

UTAH

When the Wright family was traveling in Arizona the month before, they went mining in a cave. It was a special *salted cave* which had minerals added into certain areas. They saw bats and cave formations, almost got trapped inside, and found a mysterious object. The object was black on one side and bronze on the other side, yet there were no seams. The colors blended into each other, changing gradually. The device looked like it might be an MP3 player, but it had no holes. It was about two inches square and a half of an inch thick. All the corners were rounded and smooth. It was cool to touch and had faint metallic symbols on the bronze side which had appeared shortly after they had taken it out of the cave. It had had an interestingly shaped turtle on it when they had first found it. It seemed to them like the turtle only appeared when the device had been stored away for a day or more, because within minutes after they got it out of storage different shaped objects appeared while the turtle disappeared. The black side looked like pure onyx, but it wasn't a mineral. Or, at least they didn't think it was.

Nadia and her dad both really enjoyed learning about different languages and playing with cryptograms, so they had spent a lot of time trying to decipher the pictograms on the device. They'd learned deciphering hieroglyphs was a lot harder than a language with an alphabet. They were looking forward to showing it to a different linguistic expert.

They had e-mailed Dr. Maeve Smith photographs of the glyphs on their object, yet she hadn't had time to look at them yet. Her husband, Dr. Arte Smith, was a paleontologist from a museum of archeology and paleontology and was coming to Utah in order to visit the dinosaur dig. The two lived in New York, but were rarely home since they traveled so much. Nadia thought her family was a lot like Maeve and Arte now that they lived on the road.

The pick up at the airport went smoothly. On the way back to the dig Maeve, Nadia, and Arte were in the backseat of the car. This allowed them to get to know each other better.

"Dr. Smith," Nadia said to Maeve.

"Call me Maeve. I'm not much on formality."

"But, you have to call me Dr. Smith," Arte said as he laughed. "Just kidding, you can call me Arte." He smiled at the young girl. He was a jolly man who could have passed for a young and thin Santa Claus. His hair was starting to speckle white, his cheeks were rosy, and his eyes sparkled with happiness.

UTAH

"Okay." Nadia smiled back. She tucked her long red hair behind her ears. "Maeve, my dad says you know a lot about hieroglyphs. I know he e-mailed you about the strange thing we found."

"Yes, I do and, yes, he did." Maeve smiled back. She was a happy woman. Her long gray hair was in a neat French braid, her clothing was practical yet crisp and clean, and her face showed a youthfulness which was only apparent in those who found excitement in each and every new day.

"Well, I know you've been busy, but I'm hoping since you are here now you'll look at this and tell me what the markings mean." Nadia pulled the device out of her backpack and handed it over to Maeve.

Arte watched as Maeve looked it over. He asked, "Nadia, where exactly did you say you found that?"

Nadia told him the whole story.

"Can I see it?" Arte asked.

Maeve handed the device to him.

"Wow, this is really interesting," Arte said.

"I thought you'd think so," Harrison said from the driver's seat. "Robert's never seen anything like it either."

"It's like a futuristic multilingual hieroglyphic radio," Maeve said.

"But, no visible antennae," Arte confirmed as he looked it over.

"Every so often I come across Native American rock art, but this baffles me completely," Robert added from the front passenger's seat.

"You know, I know a metallurgist who would love to look at this," Arte said as he weighed the object in his hand. "I bet it has some interesting properties."

"Either that or it's a great movie prop," Maeve laughed. "You wouldn't believe how many recreated objects we see in my lab every day. Everyone is thinking they've found the next Rosetta Stone, when really it's just someone's science fair project or theater prop."

They all laughed and began to talk about the Allosaurus dig.

"Look at that soil," Arte said as he noticed the white patches of ground.

Robert pointed to a particularly large patch. "I think that one looks just like snow."

"It does," everyone agreed.

"But, it's not," Robert said. "It's actually quartz."

UTAH

"We've seen a lot of that in this area," Nadia added and they continued talking about the unique and beautiful Utah landscape.

As they were pulling into the dinosaur site, Maeve turned to Nadia. "I brought along a few special books I think will be just perfect for deciphering your pictographs. As soon as we settle in, I'll get them out and go through them with you."

"That will be wonderful!" Nadia exclaimed.

Chapter Four

Aidan and Stephanie spent their afternoon uncovering the Allosaurus fossil while Harrison and Nadia went with Robert to the airport to pick up the guests.

"This is slow progress," Stephanie said.

"Yes, it has to be so none of the fossils get hurt," Aidan said.

"Sometimes I have a hard time telling where the dinosaur fossil even is. It's amazing the paleontologists can use picks and such. Yet if they didn't they'd never find anything."

"The dinosaur bones actually do look different than the rock," Aidan said.

"How's that?" Stephanie asked as she squinted at the rocks around her.

"Well, the bones are darker. Some are black with lines showing where the blood used to be, and some have really wild colors just like the petrified trees at the Petrified Forest in Arizona."

"Really?"

"Yep," he said.

"It seems like about one in every ten rocks we see ends up being a dinosaur bone around here," Stephanie said. "I just can't tell them apart."

"There are a lot of dinosaur bones that can be found in Utah," Aidan said. "This is one of the best places to find dinosaur bones in the whole United States, maybe even the whole world."

"So, the paleontologists just randomly dig until they find something?" Stephanie asked.

"Sometimes, but not always since there are special machines that can look deep into the ground now. Although Robert says that *people* finding bones is still more reliable than the special machines."

"And they just uncover them all by hand like what we're doing?"

UTAH

"No, they also sometimes use chemicals to help uncover the bones. Robert said that the students from the university are learning how to use the chemicals later up the road from here. Can we go?"

Stephanie nodded and brushed a bit more dirt away.

A few minutes later, Aidan took off a work glove and poked his mother in the arm. "Mom, there's something funny with my tooth," he said.

Stephanie squinted into his mouth trying to see. Just then Aidan, with his ungloved hand, presented a tooth. It was a little one from the bottom of his mouth.

"I lost a tooth!" Aidan declared with a big wide grin.

"Wow! You sure did!"

"There's not any blood or anything," Aidan said. He was very experienced at losing teeth. This was the fourth one he'd lost in about four months. The first two had been the bottom front ones, and the third was one of his top front teeth. The new teeth hadn't completely grown in, so Aidan had two gaps in his mouth when he smiled.

"It's so little," Aidan's mom said as she took the tooth from him to examine it. "It seemed big when it came in." She smiled at the memory.

"I wonder if my tooth could turn into a fossil?"

"I don't know, maybe," Stephanie said as she mussed his curly brown hair.

"I want to bury it so it can turn into a human tooth fossil."

"Sure, we can do that. We should probably ask Robert or Amanda where a good place to bury it would be, so it doesn't get dug up too soon. Let's also wait until your dad and sister come back too, so you can show it to them first."

"Good idea!" Aidan took the tooth back and put it in the front pocket of his jeans. He patted it to verify it was in there deep.

The two got back to digging, picking, and brushing. Aidan showed off his missing tooth to every person who came by to check on their progress. Amanda told him of a good spot to bury the tooth later. "You'll want to bury it where there is a lot of dirt and pebbles only, rather than big rocks."

UTAH

Shortly, the Wright's car pulled up, and the group hopped out of the car. They were all ready to get to work on their various projects. They were tired of sitting still and ready for some physical labor.

Aidan jumped up and greeted them. "Look! Look!" He pointed into his mouth. "I lost a tooth while you were gone!" He smiled proudly and showed off his new gap.

"Wow, Aidan, that's awesome!" Harrison said. He looked to Arte and Maeve. "This is my son, Aidan, and here comes Stephanie."

Stephanie stretched up and took off her gloves. She walked over to the newcomers, and shook hands with them. "It's so nice to see you again. It's been quite some time."

Aidan had Nadia over to the side of the adults. He was showing off the actual tooth which had fallen out of his mouth. "It felt funny all of a sudden, so I took off my glove and POP! It just fell into my hand," he continued saying.

Nadia handed the tooth back. "It's so little and there's no root left to it."

"I know. It didn't even bleed. It was just freaky awesome."

"Let me see your gap. Smile for me," Nadia said.

Wright ✼n Time

Aidan smiled big.

"Uh, Aidan, I thought you said you lost a bottom tooth. Your other front tooth is gone too!" Nadia squealed with excitement.

"It is?" Aidan felt around with his tongue. "Oh, wow, it is! I wondered why my mouth felt so freaky weird."

"I can't believe you lost two teeth just while we were gone! They weren't even that loose, were they?"

He shook his head. "They really weren't! Oh, this is so exciting!" He started jumping up and down.

The two ran over to their parents, who had gone ahead to the dig site with their guests and Robert.

The kids both hollered, "Mom! Dad! Another tooth is gone too. Don't dig. We have to find the missing tooth."

Robert was confused. "But, you just showed us the tooth." He pointed. "Did you drop it over there or just now?"

"Neither," Aidan said.

"He still has that tooth," Nadia said. "He just lost another one!"

"Another one?" Stephanie kneeled down to examine Aidan's mouth. "But, I just looked in there and that top tooth was there."

UTAH

"It's not now." Aidan smiled even bigger. This was turning into an extremely exciting day. He'd never heard of anyone who was lucky enough to lose two teeth in one day. He wondered if the Tooth Fairy would bring him something extra special for that. He hoped so.

Harrison peeked into his son's mouth as well. Aidan didn't realize his mouth could be such an interesting place for people to look.

"Where do you think the missing tooth is?" his father asked.

"When do you think you lost it?" Nadia asked.

"Did you have it when you went over to greet everyone?" Stephanie asked.

"I don't know. I don't know. I don't know," Aidan said. "I sound just like a parrot."

"Should we look around a bit?" Arte asked.

Aidan nodded and looked a little worried. "I don't want the tooth or anything, but do you think the Tooth Fairy will come if I don't have my tooth under my pillow? I was going to wait until tomorrow before I buried the first one I lost. I figured I could leave the Tooth Fairy a note telling her my plan."

"Definitely she'll leave something whether your tooth is under your pillow or not," Stephanie said as she assured him with a hug.

"The Tooth Fairy does different things for children who lose teeth all around the world," Maeve added.

"Really?" Aidan asked.

The adults nodded, yet continued to look for the missing tooth.

"In my family, we always put our lost teeth into glasses of water. The tooth was always replaced with a coin by the next day," Arte said.

"My mother's family is from Japan," Amanda said, "so we always buried our upper teeth and threw our bottom teeth on the roof of our house. It was considered good luck and helped the new teeth grow in properly. That's basically what you are suggesting to do with the tooth you still have, Aidan."

"I wonder if any of the baby teeth you buried are fossils," Aidan said.

"I don't think I'm quite that old," Amanda laughed.

After a while Robert said, "With all these rocks, I don't think we're ever going to find it."

"I agree," Aidan said. "Thanks for helping me look for my tooth, but it's okay if we don't find it, as long as the Tooth Fairy knows what happened."

"Do you think you might have swallowed it?" Nadia asked.

UTAH

"Maybe," he said.

The two kids looked worried.

"Will he be okay if he did?" Nadia asked her parents.

"No worries," Stephanie said. "Swallowing teeth happens all the time."

"Really?" Aidan asked.

"Yep, really," Stephanie said.

"Well, I'm the only one I know who could ever say he might have swallowed a tooth. I can't wait to tell Connor."

"I can't wait to tell Grandpa, Grandma, and Kestrel and all," Nadia added. She always liked to relay their stories to her grandparents and cousins.

"Look at me now! I'm the Holey Wonder. I've got a whole lot holes in my mouth," Aidan yelled. His smile was huge and happy. "I've got to have a straw. Gotta test these holes while I still have them," he said.

Nadia and Aidan ran around a bit, enjoying their energy and the beautiful day.

All of a sudden, Aidan stopped. "I wonder if I have any more loose teeth," he said as he felt around his mouth with his tongue.

Chapter Five

While pouring through the ancient language books Maeve had brought along, Nadia's happiness grew. She loved doing research and hadn't found anything like these amazing books at their current local library or online.

Nadia had copied the five visible symbols into her notebook just as she saw them on the device. They were lined up in a column, with one symbol on top of the other, and all were centered on the coppery side of the black object. The first was a bird, which her mom had

pegged as Egyptian. The second was a small simple square spiral Nadia believed might be Native American. It reminded her of Native American petroglyphs they'd recently seen on rocks at the Petrified Forest. The third was a roundish shape with lines inside of it. Nadia and her dad thought it might be Mayan. It reminded her of a rainbow sitting on a cloud with a pillar in the background. It was the symbol they'd seen first when the turtle symbol had disappeared. The fourth and fifth were definitely Chinese calligraphy and they sat side by side.

UTAH

"This symbol here," Maeve pointed to the bird-like image, "can have a variety of different meanings. See all the variations of birds?" Maeve pointed to a page with a bunch of different bird images on it. "Some are just a difference in the writing styles of the people who made the symbols. It's much like the handwriting differences between you and me. While we can both read each other's writing, the way we write our letters are not identical."

"So what do you think our bird means?" Nadia asked.

"Well, let's see. It is definitely Egyptian in origin. It is standing erect, facing left, has small wings, a tiny beak, and big feet. Hmm. My best guess would be that it means *travel* or *travel freely*. However," Maeve pointed to the spiral, "since the bird is right on top of this spiral, I'd guess it actually might mean traveling over a great deal of time. Maybe like a trip, like the one you and your family are taking right now. Spirals generally have a meaning of *time*."

"In all cultures?" Nadia asked.

"Actually, a spiral often means *water* in some Indian cultures," Maeve said.

"Hmm," Nadia said. "Maybe our object is a clock or some sort of stop watch or alarm clock."

Wright ✵n Time

"It definitely is small enough to be a travel clock. It's odd there are no manufacturer's markings," Maeve noticed as she looked the device over again.

"It's also weird that it seems to be solid. I mean, it doesn't look like it was made in a factory and assembled," Nadia said.

"Yet, the only way it seemed like it could have been made is in a mold. It feels as light as plastic, but it is solid like metal. It certainly is interesting." Maeve held the device, turned it around in her hands, and felt its light weight.

"I know. It's really weird," Nadia said. "I want to contact the metallurgist Arte was talking about."

"Definitely," Maeve said. "I'll have Arte e-mail him later tonight."

"Oh, that's great! Thanks for helping me decipher these symbols, too."

"It's definitely my pleasure. I don't think I've ever seen any modern day object which is so intriguing."

Nadia went back to the hieroglyph book she was in the middle of scanning. She was looking for more birds. "This one just means bird," she said. "How can you tell the difference?"

"Shape, size, orientation, and a combination of what characters are all together. It's really quite complicated and it isn't my specialty, but I do love to dabble."

UTAH

"What is your specialty?" Nadia asked.

"Celtic languages."

"That sounds interesting."

"I think so." Maeve smiled. "It's in my blood," she said. "My grandparents were from Ireland."

The two became quiet as they continued to scour the books. Maeve was typing notes of her own into her laptop. She was happy the wireless internet extended clear out to the dig site.

"This third symbol is definitely Mayan in origin," Maeve announced breaking the silence.

"That was my guess!" Nadia said.

"Wonderful! What made you think of it?" Maeve asked.

"I think it was the roundness of the shape. The way it looks like it would make a nice rubber stamp. Mostly the curviness of the whole thing felt Mayan. The Egyptian hieroglyphs aren't as smooth. They are more rigid and precise. They are certainly pretty, but different. The Mayan ones always look almost playful to me, but the Egyptian ones are more formal."

"Good observations. It was definitely artists who drew the glyphs in both civilizations."

"It would have to be!" Nadia said.

"So if the bird combined with the spiral means something like *travel freely through time*, what could the next symbols mean?" Maeve asked. "Do you have any guesses?"

"Well, these last two together are definitely Chinese in origin."

"Yes."

"Do you know any Chinese?" Nadia asked hopefully.

"I really don't except for a few special characters. I don't have any reference materials on Chinese characters and I've already looked up *time*, *clock*, *travel*, *watch*, and *hour* online, thinking that those might be right because of the meanings of the first symbols. Nothing matches even close."

"None are even close?" Nadia asked.

"I'm just not sure and I want to be completely correct before I say definitively. I do have a friend who is studying Chinese symbolism. I might have to give her a ring."

"That'd be great!" Nadia said.

UTAH

Harrison, Stephanie, and Aidan came into the tent to rest and catch up on what Maeve and Nadia had discovered.

"You all look dirty and tired," Maeve said to the lot. "Did Robert and Arte stay out there?"

"No, they went off to look at part of an Allosaurus skull that is being dug up down the road," Harrison said.

"We just needed a short break," Stephanie said.

"I didn't," Aidan said.

"I bet you didn't! You're just a little bundle of energy, aren't you?" Maeve asked him.

Aidan nodded. "Sure am!"

"Any more loose teeth in there?" Maeve asked.

"Actually, yes. But I hope I don't lose them too soon, or I won't be able to eat anything except shakes and smoothies."

"That would be so weird, Aidan. We really do need to get you some straws. I can't believe you are losing so many teeth all at once," Nadia said.

"Definitely *freaky weird*," Maeve said picking up on Aidan's vernacular as she finished sending her e-mail to her friend about the unknown meaning of the mysterious Chinese symbols.

Chapter Six

"So have you figured out any of the symbols?" Harrison asked as he sat down on a folding chair.

Nadia and Maeve had been sitting on opposite sides of a small square folding table. Stephanie took the remaining chair. Aidan danced in circles around them singing a little tune he'd made up.

"*Oh, losing loose teeth. Oh, losing loose teeth. I like to have you so I can eat! Oh losing loose teeth,*" Aidan sang.

Maeve smiled at the boy. "I remember when mine were that small, now they are in their late twenties.

Seems like yesterday. I hope you are appreciating how quickly it all goes." She looked from Stephanie to Aidan. "Much too quickly."

"We are," Stephanie replied thoughtfully.

"Good." Maeve responded and was quiet a moment. "Well, this young lady and I deciphered the first two symbols."

"Wow, that was quick!" Stephanie said.

"It sure helped that Maeve knows her way around these books," Nadia said.

Harrison picked one up and started glancing through it.

"*Please let me eat. Loose teeth, Looooose teeeeeth,*" Aidan bowed as he finished up his song. Everyone clapped.

"So, what do they mean?" Harrison asked once the clapping had subsided.

"Travel freely through time," Nadia simply stated.

"Travel freely through time," Harrison repeated.

"Travel freely through time? What could that mean?" Stephanie asked.

"Ay! There's the rub," Maeve said, quoting one of her favorite Shakespeare lines.

"We think maybe it's some kind of clock or maybe a travel alarm or stop watch," Nadia said.

UTAH

"Show me!" Aidan said suddenly. He stopped dancing and quickly joined the group at the table.

Nadia held out the device and pointed at the different symbols. "See? The bird means *travel* or *travel lightly* in Egyptian. The spiral means *time*."

"What about the freaky weird shape?" Aidan asked as he pointed at the Mayan symbol.

"We haven't figured that one out yet. I was just about to look up some possibilities." Maeve started typing again into her computer.

"Wow, you have a great battery on your laptop," Stephanie noted. "How long have you had it on out here? It must have been at least an hour or two."

Maeve looked at her battery control panel. It was still reading one hundred percent. "I better turn it off soon. I don't think my indicator lights are working properly. I usually can get two hours, but after an hour it always reads at least fifty percent gone. I'll just finish looking this up real quick and then we'll go and join Robert and Arte."

"Good! I want to see the chemicals and I want to bury my tooth," Aidan said as he held up his tooth again.

Maeve went to a website and entered something. It immediately popped up.

"I'm so impressed with the internet connection here," she said to them.

"What do you mean?" Stephanie leaned over Maeve's shoulder. "There isn't any wireless service out here at all."

"There isn't even cell phone service available, which is why we have walkie-talkies," Harrison added.

"What do *you* mean? The service is excellent! Even quicker than at home!" Maeve showed them the high speeds she was getting.

"We tried Aidan's and my laptop last week because I wanted to do some research of my own out here. Robert told us there is no satellite or cell tower that reaches this area," Nadia said. She looked at her mom. "Hey computer expert Mom, why is it working for Maeve when it didn't work for me?"

"I don't know," Stephanie said. With Maeve's permission, she looked around at a few settings, but found nothing out of the ordinary. All settings showed that the computer was connected. "We'll have to bring one of our laptops out here tomorrow," she said to Nadia.

"Definitely," Nadia said.

UTAH

With a strange silence from everyone, except Aidan, they quietly packed up their belongings and drove to the dig site where all the action was going on.

Chapter Seven

"Knock, knock," Maeve said as they all entered the large tent. Along with Robert and Arte, there was a group of about a dozen other people, including Amanda.

"Hi, Wright family. Hi, Maeve," Robert said. "Come and see this, Aidan!"

The boy rushed over to Robert's side. He was excited to see something new.

Amanda squatted down and whispered to Aidan. "How much did you uncover of the furcula today?"

Wright 🕰 n Time

"I'd say a good ten percent." Aidan was showing off his new knowledge of how a dinosaur dig actually worked.

"That's fantastic!"

"Yeah, and check this out!" He showed Amanda how he could stick his tongue through the big gap on the top of his mouth while the rest of his teeth were closed tight.

"Hey that's neat! I've told everyone about your missing tooth," she said.

"I lost two and I might have swallowed the second one." He said this part loudly and gathered the attention of the whole tent. Seeing he had, he proudly displayed his holey mouth for all to see.

"Neat-o."

"Cool."

"Wow."

Aidan's happiness was contagious.

After all had seen his mouth, Robert got them back to work. "As I was saying, we are now going to apply a special solution of plastic and solvent. Amanda will carefully brush it onto the Allosaurus fragilis left dentary."

"The Super-cali-fragil-istic-expi-ali-docious?" Nadia asked.

UTAH

The room laughed.

Robert continued, "No, Mary Poppins, the Allosaurus fragilis left dentary. That's the lower jaw. As we can currently see, this specimen has some fully erupted teeth, some partially erupted teeth, and some teeth which were just popping out of their sockets. This is an exciting find."

"Sounds like my mouth!" Aidan exclaimed.

"It sure does," Robert agreed and continued on. "We want to make sure we don't harm the jaw, so we are protecting it by making it stronger. The plastic will harden the fossil, making it stronger as the solvent evaporates."

"How big will the fossil be?" Aidan asked.

"This one appears to be about a foot in length and four or five inches tall."

"So, it's about the same size as the furcula?"

"Yes," Robert replied.

They all watched as Amanda finished applying the solution.

"After the solution is dry," Robert continued, "we'll work in two hour shifts until a significant portion of the dentary is exposed. Please let Amanda know when you are available."

Nadia quickly became uninterested in the lecture and motioned for her dad to step outside the tent.

"Think we could work together with Maeve on the Mayan symbols some more?" Nadia asked. "I want to know what the turtle symbol means, too, and I can show her the drawing I made of it."

"Probably, but we should wait to ask her until after Robert is done showing his students what to do on the fossil."

"Probably." Nadia looked disappointed.

Harrison put his arm around Nadia. "Let's take a walk."

The sun was setting in a vibrant pink. The sight was shocking compared to the dirt they'd been staring at all afternoon. They stood in silence as the pinks grew brighter, spread, and then faded to dusty purples as the sun retreated.

"You know what?" Harrison asked. "I'm starving."

"Me too," Nadia replied.

As if sensing their hunger, a catering truck pulled up with supper for the whole crew. Harrison and Nadia joined everyone for the meal. As they were finishing with their beans and rice, with extra hot sauce on the side for Harrison, Nadia went and sat next to Maeve.

UTAH

"Maeve, do you think we could figure out the Mayan symbols tonight?"

"I've already started. There is something strange about that one and I just can't stop thinking about it."

Chapter Eight

"Where's the device?" Nadia asked her dad.

"I think I left it on the dashboard of the car. We were in a hurry to get here, so I must have left it there. The car's not locked."

Nadia rushed to get it. She wanted to compare the pictures in Maeve's book to the actual symbols on the device. She wanted to double check her drawings she had created for accuracy.

A full moon had risen in the east and she was able to see particularly well on her way to the car despite the lack of lighting. Nadia opened the passenger side door and sat in the front seat. The car's overhead light turned on when she opened the door. She immediately saw the device and she picked it up. Holding it carefully, she slammed the car door shut.

Something caught her eye as she walked toward the tent. It was a glowing light and the glowing was coming from her hand. It stopped her in her tracks and she instinctively let out a scream and threw it down to the ground as though it might burn her hand. However, it hadn't been hot at all. She looked down at it and then picked it up to examine it again. Although she could see fairly well, the moonlight made both sides of the object look black—yet the symbols on it were radiating an orange glow. It was the exact orange of the flames of a fire. The harder she stared, the brighter the symbols became. Soon, they were a bright blue-white and new orange symbols appeared around the original ones.

"Dad, Mom, come quick!" Nadia yelled.

Within seconds, Nadia was surrounded by her family, along with Maeve and Arte, and Robert and Amanda.

"What's wrong?" her mom asked, scared she had been hurt by something.

"Look!" Nadia held up the device for them to see.

UTAH

Robert was holding a flashlight. He shone the light directly on the object, and all its seemingly internal light vanished.

"Turn it off," Nadia commanded. She was scared the glow wouldn't return.

Click. The flashlight snapped off.

They all stood silently around Nadia and watched the device and the amazing light show it was giving off. The blue-white was strong and steady and the orange of the outer symbols grew brighter and brighter until they, too, had turned blue-white.

"May I take a look?" Harrison asked.

Nadia immediately handed the device to her father.

"Wow. This is incredible," his voice was barely above a whisper.

"Is it hot?" Aidan asked as he reached out a finger to touch it.

"It's not," Nadia answered.

"What is it doing?" Stephanie asked. She stepped closer to Harrison and studied the new information on the device. "The new symbols are arrows."

"Arrows?" Aidan asked.

"Oh! It must be a remote control!" Stephanie said with resolve. "How handy. The symbols look just like the play, fast forward, rewind, and pause/stop buttons on a DVD player. It glows in the dark so you can find it if you've lost it. I can't believe we hadn't noticed this before."

"Oh, you're right, Mom. It does look like a remote control," Nadia said, a little disappointed but a lot more relaxed. "Do you think this is a DVD player's remote control? Or maybe a Universal remote?"

"I'm not sure," Stephanie said.

"But, it stopped glowing when I had the flashlight on it," Robert reminded them.

"That makes sense," Arte said. "I mean, you wouldn't need it to glow so much if you could see it."

"True," Robert replied.

"But, I found it in the dark and it didn't glow then," Aidan said.

"Also true," Harrison said.

"Maybe it's an *m-n-m-o-p*?" Aidan asked.

"A what?" Harrison questioned.

"You know, like that scorpion in the cave in Arizona. An *m-n-m-o-p*."

"I think you mean anomaly, since it was weird that it glowed," Nadia said.

"Yeah, freaky weird. One of those omleys, however you say it," he said with a nod.

UTAH

"Maybe it wasn't charged up, I still don't know its power source," Stephanie wondered. She took the device and looked at the other side. It was still completely black.

Nadia reached out to take the object back. "One thing I know for sure," she said, "we absolutely have to decipher the rest of the symbols now."

"I agree," Maeve said. "That device certainly is a fun mystery."

After everyone had a chance to look at the object in the moonlight, they went back into the tent to eat dessert with images of the glowing symbols lingering in their heads.

Chapter Nine

Inside the tent, Stephanie took Robert aside. "I thought there was no internet connection here," she said.

"That's right. Also, there is no electricity except from the generators, and no cell phone reception. We're really in the middle of nowhere, except the dinosaur fossils, that is. That's why we use walkie-talkies. They're the only thing which works." He nodded patiently.

"That's what I thought you'd say. But, Maeve's laptop had amazing reception back at the furcula tent."

"What?"

"It's true. I saw it myself," she said. "I can't figure it out. I saw the student taking notes on his laptop earlier. He certainly didn't have reception. I could see he wished he did."

"Right. We'd all love it," Robert said. "It would be amazing to send out photos and conduct on-the-fly research."

"Look at them!" Stephanie pointed toward Maeve and Nadia. "Do they look like they can't research anything right now?"

"Maeve must have a data library on her computer's hard drive."

"She does, but she isn't accessing her research right now and she told me she sent an e-mail earlier."

Robert and Stephanie walked to the others. They watched over Maeve's shoulder as she searched for the meaning of the specific Mayan symbol which was currently on the device.

Nadia was making fervent notes in her journal.

"Are you accessing a different computer right now?" Stephanie asked Maeve.

"Yes, I am. I'm on my home-work network."

"How is this possible?" Robert asked excitedly. He knew a bit about computers, but he wasn't an expert like Stephanie.

UTAH

"I have no idea. Do you have another laptop around here we could try?" Stephanie said.

"Yes, I'll get Amanda's, but it's probably nearly out of power."

As Robert went to get Amanda's computer, Stephanie sat with her family. Aidan was busy watching the graduate students slowly further expose the jaw bone.

"Found it, or at least something extremely similar," Maeve announced.

Everyone peered over her shoulder at the image. Sure enough, it was a Mayan symbol which looked like a little rainbow with two clouds, or pots of gold, at each end. There was the same pillar in the middle and a little pond in the front. Nadia held up her drawing for comparison and Harrison held up the device, which was still showing the regular symbols and the new remote control looking ones. The image on the computer was a bit more precise than Nadia's drawing, but a little less precise than the actual image on the device.

"That's definitely it!" Nadia said jumping up unable to control her excitement.

"What's it called?" Harrison wanted to know.

"What's it mean?" Nadia asked.

"It says here that it means *year*. I see several definitions of what *year* means for this specific usage of the symbol,

Wright in Time

but basically it means the time it takes for the Earth to complete a revolution around the Sun."

"So in order from top to bottom the symbols mean *travel freely*, *time*, *year*, and we don't know the bottom Chinese symbols yet," Maeve said.

"Don't forget to add in the remote control symbols of *pause/stop*, *play*, *fast forward*, and *rewind*," Nadia said.

"And the turtle symbol," Stephanie said.

"Oh, yes, I found that one already. The middle of the turtle, or his shell, is a *Hunab Ku* symbol which represents balance. I don't know why it's on the shell of a turtle though," Maeve said.

"Well, anyway, those other symbols sound like a stop watch," Harrison said.

"They sure appear to be," Maeve agreed.

Aidan heard their excitement and came to join them. "So, the rainbow thing means *year*?" he asked.

"Yes," Nadia said.

"What's the new symbol called?" Harrison asked again.

"Well, calling exact symbols precise names is always a bit of a challenge." Maeve scrolled through a few pronunciation guides. "Looks like either *tun*, pronounced like the music word *tune*, or *ja'ab*, pronounced like *ja* with an *ahb*."

"Tune?" Aidan latched on to that word. "It's a Time Tuner," he joked.

"Time Tuner? That's funny!" Maeve said.

"Seems appropriate if it's a stop watch," Stephanie said.

"A bit grandiose, but that works for us," Harrison agreed.

"It would be nice to call it something other than 'that mystery device' or 'that thing we found in the cave'," Nadia agreed.

"Time Tuner it is then," Harrison declared.

"So, Time Tuner," Stephanie spoke to the device as she examined it again, "just what in the world is your purpose?"

The arrows had slowly disappeared and the glowing had abruptly stopped when they had taken the Time Tuner into the tent. Only the original symbols, in their original black, now remained.

"I want to see it glow again," Aidan said.

"Me too," Nadia said.

"Me three," Harrison joined in.

The three left Stephanie and Maeve at Maeve's computer while they went outside to see if the device would glow again.

Suddenly, Maeve announced, "That's weird, or as Aidan would say, that's *freaky weird*."

"What is?" Stephanie asked.

Maeve pointed to the indicator lights on her computer. "Oh, I haven't had my computer plugged in all day. I bet that is why it is acting all strange."

Stephanie noticed the connectivity light flashing, and the computer's battery light showed it was running low on battery.

"Hmm," Stephanie agreed, "that is strange."

Robert walked up to the two women from the other side of the tent carrying Amanda's laptop.

"I checked Amanda's computer," he said. "No reception. I think Maeve's computer must have a built in access point or router or something. There must be a satellite I don't know about. I'm definitely going to get a satellite receiver soon and see if I can get reception out here, too."

"Hmm." Stephanie was still thinking out loud.

"Well, it's not working now," Maeve said. "But, when it was working, it was faster than I'd ever seen it before."

UTAH

The kids burst back into the tent.

"It's glowing again!" Aidan hollered.

"Same markings as before," Nadia said. "See?" She held up the device to her mom. Within seconds, the glowing faded and the extra symbols completely disappeared, leaving the device to look as though the extra symbols had never existed.

"Look!" Robert pointed at Maeve's laptop. "She's at full power again and has an internet connection again."

"Exactly as I thought," Stephanie announced. "It seems to be the Time Tuner."

"Huh?" Aidan asked.

"Our little Time Tuner seems to have special properties that I've never seen before. It seems to be charging Maeve's laptop and allowing it to connect to the Internet."

"How is that possible?" Harrison asked with amazement.

"I don't know for sure," Stephanie said, "but I definitely want to try and find out!"

"Quick, let's try Amanda's laptop again," Robert said. He opened the laptop and sure enough, it worked better than it ever had. Not only that, but the battery light was off and the machine indicated it was at one hundred percent power.

"This device seems to power everything around it," Stephanie said.

"Now, how is that possible?" Harrison asked doubtingly. "It's not even connected to anything."

"This is so exciting!" Nadia said. "I wonder who made the Time Tuner and how and why it was left in a cave in Arizona."

"Now that is an excellent question!" Stephanie said.

Chapter Ten

As had become their daily custom, Aidan and Nadia greeted their pet turtle as they rushed into their RV home that evening.

"Prince Pumpkin the Third! Prince Pumpkin the Third!" The two hollered into the main room.

Prince Pumpkin the Third lifted his head up high, exposing his neck, as the kids took the lid off his terrarium. The medium sized turtle enjoyed having his neck lightly rubbed.

"I lost two teeth today!" Aidan told the turtle.

"He didn't even know about the second one. It just popped out! I wonder what the person who finds it will think," Nadia added.

"Unless I swallowed it," Aidan added.

Prince Pumpkin III stared at the children, moving his head back and forth between them as if understanding their conversation.

"And, that's not it for all the excitement today! The device glowed! And we think we figured out three of the symbols! They mean *travel freely through time of a year.* I don't know what it means yet, but there are still the Chinese symbols for us to decipher," Nadia rattled off.

"And, don't forget the Allosaurus furcula," Aidan interrupted.

"Yes, a real dinosaur wishbone."

"But that glowing was freaky weird!"

"Yes, it was. This has got to be the best day ever," Nadia remarked.

"Definitely," Aidan agreed.

The turtle nodded in agreement.

UTAH

Later before bed Aidan, with Nadia's help, wrote Connor a quick e-mail.

Dear Connor,

I now have bigger gaps in my mouth! I lost two teeth in one day. I probably even swallowed one of them. Isn't that freaky cool? I can't wait to see what the Tooth Fairy brings me.

I helped uncover a furcula from an Allosaurus today. It's a wishbone in a dinosaur. It shows that they might have been related to birds. I also got to see this freaky weird plastic stuff that makes fossils harder while they are being dug out. It was really neat.

And just so you know, Arizona doesn't have a state dinosaur! Nadia looked it up for me. Apparently some people wanted it to be the Sonorasaurus thompsoni, but it was never passed in a vote. I'm disappointed, but maybe we'll get one eventually. But, we do have a state fossil, it's petrified wood.

I will write you again soon! I miss you and hope I get to see you before we're back in Arizona again.

Wright On Time

Maybe you could visit me somewhere? I'll ask my mom to send your mom our plans.

Your best friend,
Aidan

THE END

GLOSSARY

algae [**al**-gee]; type of water plant.

Allosaurus fragilis [al-uh-**sohr**-uhs] [**fra**-jil-uhs];
Utah's state dinosaur. It was a large and smart carnivore
which lived in the late Jurassic period and walked on
two legs. Up to 16.5 feet tall, 38 feet long, and 1400
kilograms.

archeology [ahr-kee-**ahl**-*uh*-jee]; careful study of past human life and cultures by examining found evidence.

Barringer Crater [**bare**-ihn-jer] [**kray**-ter]; specific crater found in Northern Arizona, it rises 150 feet above ground level, is almost a mile wide, and it is 570 feet deep.

Celtic [**kel**-tik]; of the Celts or their languages, currently located in Ireland, the Scottish Highlands, Wales, and Brittany.

conspiratorial [k*uh*n-spir-*uh*-**tor**-ee-*uhl*]; secret plan formulated by two or more people.

crater [**krey**-ter]; bowl shaped depression in the ground.

cryptogram [**krip**-t*uh*-gram]; secret writing in a code or cipher.

data library [**dey**-t*uh*, **dat**-*uh*] [**li**-brar-ee]; individual facts, statistics, or items of information about a particular topic. *Dr. Maeve Smith had a data library on her computer with linguistic information.*

UTAH

debug [dee-**buhg**]; to detect and remove errors from (a computer program). *Stephanie Wright debugged her computer program.*

decipher [deh-**sie**-fer]; to discover the meaning of an object. *Nadia helped decipher the strange markings on the mysterious device.*

dentary [**den**-tuh-ree]; lower jaw. The paleontologists found the left dentary of a dinosaur.

Egyptian [ee-**jipt**-shuhn]; of the people from Egypt or their languages.

fervent [**fur**-vent]; having or showing lots of excitement for something.

Four corners; spot where four states meet at one point. The four states are Arizona, Utah, Colorado and New Mexico.

freaky awesome, freaky cool, freaky weird; fun phrases Aidan Wright is popularizing. *Aidan saw a really neat object. "Freaky cool!" he said.*

freelance writer; the job of a writer who works alone and is contracted for specific writing assignments. *Harrison Wright is a freelance writer.*

furcula [fur-ky*uh*-l*uh*]; wish bone, the forked collar bone of a bird or dinosaur. *The Allosaurus fragilis has a furcula. Aidan helped uncover one.*

futuristic [fyoo-ch*uh*-**ris**-tik]; pertaining to the future.

generator [**jen**-*uh*-rey-ter]; machine which converts one type of energy into another.

glyph [glif]; pictograph or hieroglyph.

grandiose; [**gran**-dee-ohs]; splashy and important.

hard drive; part of a computer's hardware which holds most of the information.

hieroglyph [hie-ro-**glif**]; having to do with a symbol which is a picture which represents a word or sound.

homeschool [hohm-skool]; educated at home. *The Wright children are homeschooled.*

UTAH

linguistics [ling-**gwis**-tiks]; the science of languages.

Mayan [**mah**-y*uh*n]; of the Maya people or their languages, located in Central and South America.

metallurgist [**met**-ah-**lur**-jist]; person who works with metals.

MP3 player; device which plays music and other audio files.

multilingual [muhl-tie-**ling**-gw*uhl*]; able to speak more than one language with ease.

paleontology [pey-lee-*uh*n-**tahl**-*uh*-jee]; study of life existing in former geological periods, using fossils.

pictograph [**pik**-t*uh*-graf]; a picture or symbol that represents a word.

pictogram [**pik**-t*uh*-gram]; See pictograph.

prehistoric [pree-hi-**stor**-ik]; before written history, like when dinosaurs roamed the earth.

recreational vehicle (RV); large vehicle that people can travel and live in. *The Wright family live in an RV.*

revolution [rev-*uh*-**loo**-sh*uh*n]; the orbiting of one object around another.

Rosetta Stone; a tablet found in 1799 which provided key information to deciphering hieroglyphs.

runestone [roon-stohn]; stone or rock with drawings or inscriptions, often with a mysterious meaning.

salted cave; special cave that has had minerals, fossils, or other interesting objects planted for people to find.

satellite (receiver) [**sat**-uh-lite]; man-made device which was launched into space and orbits the Earth, allowing communication to be more efficient.

specimen [**spes**-*uh*-m*uh*n]; a sample of an object that is studied and examined.

solvent [**sol**-v*uh*nt]; substance that dissolves another substance to form a solution.

UTAH

Supercalifragilisticexpialidocious   [soo-per-cal-ih-fraj-ihl-is-tik-eks-pee-a-lee-doh-shus]; famous Mary Poppins song, written by the Sherman brothers.

symposium [sim-**poh**-zee-*uh*m]; A meeting or conference where several speakers talk or discuss a particular topic. *Dr. Maeve Smith went to a linguistics symposium before she met the Wright family in Utah.*

telecommute [**tel**-i-k*uh*-myoot]; to work at home using a computer that is connected to a company's network.

Time Tuner; amazing device the Wright family found in a salted cave in Southern Arizona, properties currently unknown.

vernacular [ver-**nak**-y*uh*-ler]; a style of language which is specific to a place or group of people. *Aidan Wright has a particular vernacular that includes the word 'freaky' frequently.*

zooplankton; [zoh-*uh*-plangk-tuhn]; really small animal-like masses which live in water.

MORE FACTS ABOUT UTAH

- Highest Point: Kings Peak, 13,528 feet above sea level
- Lowest Point: Beaver Dam Wash, 2000 feet above sea level
- Size: 84,889 square miles (13th largest state)
- Residents are called: Utahans or Utahns
- 45th state to officially become a state
- Largest Lake: Great Salt Lake
- Bordering States: Arizona, Colorado, Idaho, Nevada, New Mexico, Wyoming
- State Cooking Pot: Dutch Oven
- State Dance: Square Dance
- State Fish: Bonneville Cutthroat Trout
- State Fruit: Cherry
- State Gem: Topaz
- State Grass: Indian Rice Grass
- State Motto: "Industry"
- State Rock: Coal

What is that image the Wright family saw on the *mysterious* device?

In Arizona, the Wright family finds a *mysterious* device which shows an image of a turtle with a special symbol in the middle. The symbol is based off of an ancient Mayan glyph called a **Hunab Ku** symbol. The Mayans believed that the symbol represented the gateway to other galaxies beyond our own sun. Only the maker of the device understands why the Hunab Ku was drawn inside of a turtle. Check out **www.WrightOnTimeBooks. com** and read *Wright on Time: WYOMING, Book 3* to find out more!

Hey, Kids & Parents!

Have you been on any fun trips lately? Do you have a dream vacation? Going on a trip soon and looking for fun things to do?

Where do you think the Wright family should visit next on their RV trip around the USA? Is there a really fun place they should go to in your state?

Join the Forums on **www.WrightOnTimeBooks. com** and tell us all about your trips and all the fun places you've been! If you are younger than 13, be sure to get your parent's permission first.

Thanks!
Lisa

Dear Readers,

I hope you've enjoyed this book about my family. I've started my very own blog, telling all about places we've been and things we've seen that aren't in these books. I can't tell you where we are right now since that's top secret, but there are sure to be places that we've been that you'll find interesting.

To read more, and to tell me of places my family and I should check out (I love comments), see my blog at **www.WrightOnTimeBooks.com/ nadia.** Aidan says he thinks it's freaky cool!

Love,
Nadia

CONTEST

Like this book? Want to see your name in print? The first child (13 and younger) from each state who reviews this book will have their review listed in *Wright on Time: WYOMING, Book 3*. To be considered, please post your review on the **www.WrightOnTimeBooks.com** website as a blog comment in the *Reviews* section, or e-mail Lisa directly at **reviews@WrightOnTimeBooks.com**. Don't forget to add your review to the amazon.com page, too! You'll need to include your first name, your state, your age, and your review (no more than 3 sentences if possible).

Please send Lisa your comments and questions at any time. She loves reading e-mails and seeing drawings from real kids just like you. She looks forward to hearing your thoughts and ideas!

Join Nadia and Aidan on their first adventure in *Wright on Time: ARIZONA, Book 1.* There the Wrights explored a salted cave. Nadia hoped to find minerals and see rock formations. Aidan really wanted to see bats. This is the adventure where the mysterious device was found. Where was it, and what does it do? Published in August 2009.

Join Nadia and Aidan as they continue their adventures in *Wright on Time: WYOMING, Book 3* coming out in 2010. The Wrights visit geysers, tour a hydroelectric water plant, fly in a private plane, and more! What will they find and what will they learn about that mysterious device? Be sure to check out **www.WrightOnTimeBooks.com** for even more fun, games, and a forum for you to post your own adventure tips!

TANJA BAUERLE is an active member of the Arizona chapter of the Society of Children's Book Writers and Illustrators and helps as Co-Illustrator Representative. After having lived in Germany and Australia, Tanja now calls Arizona home with her husband Kevin, her daughters Isabelle and Zoe, her two Goldens Otto and Peanut, and cat Ducky.

Tanja has had her own illustration and design business since 2003. Her love of story telling drives her to continually refine her craft. Her favorite mediums are acrylics, water color, and pen and ink, yet she loves digital tools also.

Check out **www.TanjaBauerle.com** for more information and to see some of her award winning work.

Photograph by Teagan Bentley, ©2009

LISA M. COTTRELL-BENTLEY has been writing since she was a child, winning her **first writing** contest at age 9. She's been writing professionally since 2002. Lisa is an active member of RWA and SCBWI.

Lisa and her daughters spent many hours searching for children's books about homeschoolers, but found very few. So, they decided to create their own. As they discussed their dream storylines, the *Wright on Time* series took shape. While they haven't found any mysterious devices *yet*, they have done lots of field research trying out many of the activities described in these books.

Lisa lives and learns while writing in southern Arizona with her husband Greg, two happy always homeschooled daughters Zoë and Teagan, and three cats. Her desire is for all people to live their own personal dreams, now and for always.

Looking for more right now? Check out
www.WrightOnTimeBooks.com!

NOTES

LaVergne, TN USA
30 July 2010
191525LV00001BA/127/P